Hail to the King!

by **Kathryn Lay**   illustrated by **Jason Wolff**

visit us at www.abdopublishing.com

To my dad for always loving me and my family— KL

Published by Magic Wagon, a division of the ABDO Group,
8000 West 78th Street, Edina, Minnesota 55439. Copyright
© 2011 by Abdo Consulting Group, Inc. International copyrights
reserved in all countries. All rights reserved. No part of this book
may be reproduced in any form without written permission from the
publisher.

Calico Chapter Books™ is a trademark and logo of Magic Wagon.

Printed in the United States of America, Melrose Park, Illinois.
032010
092010

 This book contains at least 10% recycled materials.

Text by Kathryn Lay
Illustrations by Jason Wolff
Edited by Stephanie Hedlund and Rochelle Baltzer
Cover and interior design by Abbey Fitzgerald

Library of Congress Cataloging-in-Publication Data
Lay, Kathryn.
   Hail to the king! / by Kathryn Lay ; illustrated by Jason Wolff.
      p. cm. -- (Wendy's weather warriors ; bk. 4)
   Includes bibliographical references and index.
   ISBN 978-1-60270-757-3 (alk. paper)
   1. Hailstorms--Juvenile literature. I. Wolff, Jason, ill. II. Title.
   QC929.H15L39 2010
   551.57'87--dc22
                                          2009048839

CONTENTS

CHAPTER 1

The Big Announcement

"Mr. Andrews would make the best king in all of Circleville Elementary!" Wendy said.

She held out the list of teachers who were nominated for the Spring Carnival King and Queen. There were five male and five female teachers who'd been nominated by other teachers. And now the kids got to vote.

All around her, kids were grabbing copies from the table beside the school office. Everyone had been talking about the carnival for weeks. There would be games, food, and booths. And there'd be rides, too.

Wendy and her two best friends, Dennis Galloway and Jessica Roberts, walked down the hall to Mr. Andrews's class.

Dennis waved the voting form and grinned. "Mr. Andrews would definitely be the best king. He's a good sport about crazy fun stuff."

"What does that mean?" Wendy asked. "Isn't this a good thing to win?"

"It's great. I wish I could be king. They get to rule over the carnival and sit on their special throne all day and . . ." Dennis took a deep breath and suddenly fell on the floor and shouted, "Splash!"

"Splash?" Wendy asked.

"Splash," Jessica said.

Wendy giggled. Sometimes her friends could be silly. Other times they were serious, especially when it came to weather. Today, they were silly.

"The Dunk the King/Dunk the Queen booth!" Dennis explained. "It raises the most money for the school. Sometimes people pick the teachers they like the most or the ones they don't like."

Wendy's mouth fell open. They were going to dunk the king and queen of the carnival? If anyone would have fun getting dunked, it was Mr. Andrews.

When they walked into the classroom, their teacher was standing at his desk. Bob the Boa was wrapped around his arm and kids were surrounding him.

"What's going on?" Wendy asked Lindsey Collins.

Lindsey stepped back from the kids crowding around their teacher. "Mr.

Andrews says he has a big announcement to make. Kara Dickinson said she heard someone say he might be leaving Circleville Elementary. For good."

Wendy gasped. "Leaving? But he can't. He's the best teacher ever."

Lindsey nodded. "He won't say what the big announcement is until everyone is in class and sitting down."

Wendy's heart pounded. What would they do if Mr. Andrews left? Would another teacher let the Weather Warriors talk about weather and let Dennis teach everyone exciting weather experiments? Or let Wendy bring in special videos her Dad got from his storm chasing friends?

"Everyone, please find your seats," Mr. Andrews said.

"Hurry," Wendy told them. She grabbed Jessica by the arm and pulled her to her desk. Then she ran to her own desk.

It seemed to take forever for everyone to get quiet. Mr. Andrews cleared his throat. He walked slowly to the back of the room and put Bob back into his aquarium. He cleared his throat again.

Wendy had never seen her teacher act so strange.

"I know everyone is excited about the Spring Carnival and the king and queen elections," Mr. Andrews said. "But before we get to all that and to our classwork, I have a quick announcement. You see, it's a bit of important news."

Austin Scott popped out of his seat and put his hands around his mouth. He shouted, "News! News! Call the paper, call the radio, and call the president!"

Mr. Andrews cleared his throat again. "Austin, please sit down and pay attention."

Austin slid into his seat and leaned forward, his hands pushing his ears toward Mr. Andrews.

Wendy thought she would explode if Mr. Andrews didn't tell them his news. It was like a big storm in her stomach.

"As I was saying, I have an announcement. A big announcement," Mr. Andrews said. He leaned against his desk. Then he smiled.

Wendy wondered how Mr. Andrews could smile about leaving them.

"I'd like to announce something wonderful and amazing. And something sad," Mr. Andrews said. "During spring break, I'll be looking for a new house. I've been offered a job at a school in Arizona as a vice principal next year."

Wendy held her breath. She didn't want to hear what else he had to say. But he said it anyway.

"The sad part is, I've talked to Mrs. Stuard and I am taking a leave of absence to move and get prepared. It means . . . well, it means that I won't be your teacher any longer."

Wendy looked at Jessica. It couldn't be true. But he'd said it. He was moving away before the school year ended.

Mr. Andrews was leaving Circleville Elementary.

CHAPTER 2

· Project Save Mr. Andrews ·

Wendy called an emergency meeting of the Weather Warriors after school. But this time, the emergency wasn't about weather.

Austin ran in circles while Cumulus chased him.

"Austin, please sit down," Wendy said.

He crossed his eyes at her. "We're not in school, and you're not my teacher."

Wendy wished for about the millionth time she hadn't let Austin join the Weather Warriors. Even if he had given the school a great snow party in November.

Dennis whistled for Cumulus. The Schnoodle cocked his head and licked his lips, then jumped onto Dennis's lap. Dennis reached into his pocket and pulled out a dog treat. He always brought treats for Cumulus when he came to the clubhouse.

"Dog thief!" Austin growled. He plopped onto the floor.

"Listen, we have to stop Mr. Andrews from leaving Circleville," Wendy said. "If Mr. Andrews hadn't helped us talk with Mrs. Stuard about tornado safety, someone at school would've gotten hurt. He let us watch that great video in class on lightning. And he helped with the snow party."

Jessica sat down beside Dennis and rubbed Cumulus's head. "I don't want him to leave either, but it's kind of exciting for him that he's going to be a vice principal. Isn't it?"

Wendy tapped Jessica on the knee to get her attention. "It would be exciting for some other kids in Arizona, but horrible for us. What if we get some boring teacher who just stands and talks at the board all day?

"What if we get someone who gives tests every day? Or is afraid of snakes and hamsters? Or, what if we get a teacher who doesn't care about weather at all?" she finished with a gasp for air.

Dennis pulled out his experiment notebook. "Yeah, we might get a teacher who only wants us to read about stuff, not do cool stuff. Like this experiment on stormy weather where you measure rainfall. See, you take a big soda bottle and turn it upside down. Then . . ."

Wendy slammed her hand on the clubhouse wall. "Then it's decided, we can't let him leave. We have to make sure he is crowned Spring Carnival King and has the best carnival ever. Then he'll see that he can't leave us."

Austin pulled his knees up to his chin and spun around in a circle. When he stopped spinning, he said, "I was at the mall last week and this guy was going around the parking lot sticking pieces of paper on everyone's cars. I pulled off a bunch of them."

Wendy stared at Austin. Sometimes he was really weird. And sometimes, he had great ideas. She snapped her fingers. "You are a genius, Austin."

Austin's eyebrows went up and down like exercising caterpillars. "Really?" He smiled at Wendy. "Why am I a genius?"

"Because," she said, "you gave me a super idea. Let's go inside and I'll show you what I mean."

Cumulus followed Wendy and her friends out of the clubhouse and into the house.

Her mother was cutting apples into slices. "Oh, I was just about to bring a snack to everyone."

"No time, Mom. Is it okay if we get on the computer?" Wendy asked.

Her mother stopped cutting apples. "I guess we'll have apple and raisin salad for dessert tonight. Why do you need the computer?"

Wendy explained about Mr. Andrews and her plan. Her mother smiled. "I like Mr. Andrews, too. I hope he wins."

"Thanks, Mom," Wendy said. She gave her mother a quick hug, then waved at her friends. "Come on." She led them to the computer in the living room.

Wendy turned the computer on and waited for it to hum to life. "We have to make a flyer for Mr. Andrews. We can use it to get everyone to vote for him for Spring Carnival King. Then he'll know he's too popular to leave. Ever."

"Perfect," Jessica said. "I have a picture of Mr. Andrews in my camera that we can download to put on the flyer. It's of him standing next to a snowman at the snow party."

Wendy started typing.

CHAPTER 3

Voting!

"**V**ote for Mr. Andrews for Spring Carnival King!" Austin yelled.

Wendy stuffed a flyer into the hand of every kid sitting in the cafeteria. The other kids in Mr. Andrews's class were doing the same.

"What do I get if I vote for him?" a kid standing in the lunch line asked. "I'm not even in fifth grade till next year."

"That's the reason you should vote for Mr. Andrews," Wendy explained. "He's the best teacher ever and he's talking about leaving Circleville Elementary, which means you won't have a chance of

19

getting him next year. He has a boa and a hamster in class. And we just got a lizard —Leaping Larry."

The kid's eyes bulged. "Does he really leap?"

Wendy shrugged. "You'll find out if Mr. Andrews stays for next year."

The kid nodded and grabbed a flyer.

Wendy gave out the last of her flyers. The smell of the food was making her really hungry. She went back to her seat and opened her lunch box.

She took a bite of her sandwich. "Mmm, one of Dad's special sandwiches," she said when the rest of the Weather Warriors sat down. "Cheese and jelly."

Jessica wrinkled her nose. "Eew."

Austin leaned over and sniffed Wendy's sandwich.

Dennis took a bite of his taco surprise. "Sounds better than this stuff." He mixed his mashed potatoes with the meat, took another bite and smiled. "I gave out all my flyers."

"Me too," Jessica said. "I hope the other teachers don't get their feelings hurt when Mr. Andrews wins."

Wendy shook her head. "Everyone likes Mr. Andrews. He won teacher of the year last year."

After lunch, Mr. Andrews passed out the carnival king and queen ballots, gave everyone five minutes to vote, then chose Barry Webber to take them to the office.

Wendy winked at Jessica. She couldn't wait for the announcement.

It came while everyone was sitting in the science station. Dennis was giving a list of all the types of weather that can happen in the spring.

"...and sometimes it gets cold again all of a sudden and then warm. And we can have rain showers and big storms with hail. And it gets really windy. Oh, and if I had some plastic lids and a magnifying glass and ... well, some other stuff, I could make something cool that shows what kinds of things the wind blows around and—"

Mr. Andrews pointed to a new poster on the wall behind the science station. "Good job, Dennis. Spring in this part of Texas has a wide range of changes. Last week it was seventy-five degrees one day, and forty-five the next.

"There are storm predictions for possible rain later this week, though it's warm and dry today. The trees are starting to bud and flowers are blooming, but we could still have freezing temperatures some mornings. This would damage them."

Wendy raised her hand. But just as Mr. Andrews pointed at her, the intercom crackled.

Mrs. Stuard's voice said, "I'd like to quickly announce the winners of our student voting for king and queen of the Spring Carnival. The winners are, Miss Holland, first grade Room 1A and Mr. Andrews, fifth grade Room 5C. Congratulations.

"Remember, students, please bring your parents to help build booths on Wednesday after school. Then on Thursday, five students from each fifth grade class will help set everything up

after lunch. We're expecting the carnival to be . . ."

Before Mrs. Stuard finished talking, everyone started cheering for Mr. Andrews. Wendy cheered the loudest.

Mr. Andrews laughed. "Well, looks like I'm in for some dunking. It'll give everyone a chance to get me wet the last day I'll be here."

Wendy stopped cheering. Even though he was going to be king of the carnival, Mr. Andrews was still planning on leaving Circleville. He was going to leave Room 5C.

"Wendy, would you like to talk about spring storms after you return from the holiday?" Mr. Andrews asked. "I'm sure I can leave a note for my replacement. I saw your father last week when he was buying batteries. He said he keeps them around in case of storms."

Wendy nodded. Her throat hurt too much to talk. But she forced herself to say, "Dad keeps lots of batteries around this time of year in case the electricity goes out."

Mr. Andrews nodded. "That's what I mean. You have lots of good information. In fact, maybe your father could talk to the class about being a storm spotter."

He waited for her to answer. Wendy stared at her desk. She was sure everyone was staring at her. All she wanted to say was, "please don't leave, Mr. Andrews."

Instead she forced a smile and said, "My dad would love to come."

When Mr. Andrews went back to his desk, Jessica leaned over and whispered, "Too bad Mr. Andrews won't be here to listen to your dad."

CHAPTER 4

The Idea Box

Wendy's Weather Warriors held a meeting on the playground during recess.

Austin hung upside down on the climbing bars. Everyone else sat on the swings.

"We did it," Dennis said. "Mr. Andrews is king of the carnival. I bet he decides to stay now."

Wendy folded her arms. She scraped her shoes against the dirt under her swing. "I heard him telling Mr. Grogan during lunch that he's already got a house picked out in Arizona. He's started packing."

Jessica wiped her hand across her eyes. "I don't want him to leave. Why can't he at least wait until school ends?"

"Hey, I bet we just get a bunch of substitutes the rest of the year," Austin said. He swung higher and higher.

Austin waved his hands like a monkey. "I like substitutes." He grinned, but it looked like a frown from upside down. "They don't like me though."

The bell rang and the teachers called everyone to line up to go back to class.

"We've just got to do something special to make Mr. Andrews change his mind," Wendy said. "This year's carnival has to be the best one ever. Nothing can happen to mess it up. Why would he leave such a great school?"

Dennis said, "To be a vice principal."

Wendy knew he was right, but she just couldn't let Mr. Andrews leave them.

They passed by the office on their way to class. Outside the office door was a big box wrapped in bright green foil. Wendy looked closer and saw a slot in the top of the box. On the side were the words, "Spring Carnival Ideas."

As they walked down the hall, Wendy hurried to catch up with Jessica. "We should stuff that box with amazing ideas. Things that show Mr. Andrews how much we need him. Pass the word."

Jessica nodded and tapped Joey Lang's shoulder. She whispered in his ear. He nudged the kid next to him.

Mr. Andrews stood at the door to the classroom. "There sure is a lot of talking in the hall."

Wendy squirmed in her seat while Mr. Andrews talked about Vikings during social studies.

"We've been talking about the explorers and the Vikings. Does anyone remember how a wealthy Viking was buried?" he asked.

Hands shot into the air. Wendy knew the answer, too.

"They were buried on their ship," Martha Fenner said.

Mr. Andrews nodded. "Then what happened to the ship?"

Austin jumped up and shouted, "Poof! It was burned up."

"Yes, their ships were very important to a Viking, even when they died," Mr. Andrews explained. "They were great explorers and often left home to sail the seas."

Wendy raised her hand. "Sometimes people should stay where they are, don't you think, Mr. Andrews?"

Mr. Andrews folded his arms and leaned against his desk. He smiled at Wendy. "It's exciting to try new things and see new places."

Wendy frowned.

Didn't Mr. Andrews understand he could try new things right there in Circleville? By the time the Warriors were done with the perfect carnival, he'd change his mind.

CHAPTER 5

Carnival Forecast

" **I** think Mr. Andrews should judge some kind of contest at the carnival," Dennis said. He wrote down on one of the note cards Wendy had given everyone at the clubhouse, *Mr. Andrews can judge the Best Pet Trick Contest.*

He held up his card for the others to see. Cumulus sniffed the card and sneezed.

Austin scribbled quickly on his card. He jumped up and waved it in front of Wendy's nose. She grabbed it and read, "Mr. Andrews has to eat ten hot dogs as fast as he can."

She shook her head. "It might make him sick. Then he wouldn't think the carnival was so great."

Austin grabbed the card back, made a slash over the number ten and changed it to a five. Then he added, "With catsup and green relish and onions on top."

Jessica tapped her pencil against her nose. "If we want to show him how important he is, I could take a picture and blow it up so it's really big. Then everyone can sign it, like a giant card. But they have to say only nice things."

"Kaboom!" Austin said.

Jessica gave him a little push. "Not that kind of blown up."

Wendy hugged Jessica. "That's a great idea."

She stared at her blank card. She couldn't think of anything. She tried snapping her fingers, but the perfect idea still didn't come.

"KCWS93W, Weathermouth here. Are you there, StormGirl?" a voice filled the room.

Wendy jumped up and ran to the corner table, where her ham radio sat. She grabbed the microphone and said, "This is KWP9S. StormGirl here. What's going on?"

The others came to stand beside Wendy. Austin grabbed at the microphone, but Wendy moved it away from him.

"You asked me yesterday if I thought the weather would be nice for your school carnival on Friday. We may have some rain coming in on Saturday sometime, but Friday looks to be clear. There might be a little shower on Thursday, but I think it'll come and go quickly."

Wendy shouted, "That's great! Just what I wanted to hear. Everything has to be perfect on Friday."

Weathermouth laughed. "Well, I can't guarantee that will happen, but I don't see the rain that's coming in staying for very long. Doesn't look like any tornadic weather or high winds."

"Thanks," Wendy said. "Bye, Weathermouth!"

Austin grabbed at the microphone and pulled it toward him. "Over and out. Out and over. Up and down."

Wendy pulled it back. "You don't have to say all that stuff."

She grinned at the others. "I can't think of any great ideas for Mr. Andrews to do at the carnival, but at least we can tell Mrs. Stuard that it'll be a nice day for it."

She looked outside the window and up at the clouds. "Nope, nothing to worry about this time."

CHAPTER 6

Building a Carnival

Wendy wiped a splotch of purple paint off her hands. Her old, torn pants were beginning to look like a rainbow and smell like a paint store.

She closed her eyes and could hear all the hammering around her. The school yard was crowded with kids and parents building and painting booths and signs for the carnival.

Wendy leaned over to read Jessica's sign.

ATOGRAPH MR. ANDREWS!

"That doesn't look right," Wendy said. "I think you left out a letter in autograph."

Jessica stared at it a for a minute. "Oh rats, you're right." She took white paint and painted over the whole board. "When that dries I'll paint the words again."

Wendy was painting the sign that would be above the dunk tank. She was careful to keep the purple letters straight.

"See, purple for a king," she said.

SPRING CARNIVAL KING!

She had finished painting the hamster and snake and lizard that Carla Rogers had drawn. Carla was the best artist in the fifth grade.

Mrs. Stuard walked past. She stepped back and knelt down.

"Good job, Wendy. And Jessica, that's a great photograph of Mr. Andrews.

Especially with the snake around his arm and the crown on his head. Nice touch."

Jessica's face turned red. Wendy knew that she loved compliments about her photography, even when it wasn't weather pictures.

Dennis ran over and tapped the principal on the arm. "Come quick, Mrs. Stuard. Austin hit his thumb with a hammer."

Mrs. Stuard followed Dennis across the school grounds. Wendy could hear Austin yelling.

A few minutes later, Dennis walked over with Austin following him.

"Is your thumb okay?" Wendy asked.

Austin nodded. He shoved his thumb at Wendy's face. It was wrapped in a white bandage. "Cool, huh?"

Wendy rolled her eyes and pushed his hand away. She picked up her sign and carried it carefully to where other signs were leaning to dry.

The booths were starting to look like they belonged at a real carnival. They were a little crooked and the letters weren't all the same size on the signs. But Wendy thought they looked almost perfect.

The next day the carnival rides would come. And then the food. Wendy had heard all about last year's carnival. But this one would be even more fun. This one had Mr. Andrews as king.

Wendy folded her arms. It was going to be hard to concentrate on school Thursday.

CHAPTER 7

All Hail to the Carnival

On the day before the big carnival, Wendy shivered at the sudden cold breeze. She rubbed her arms and stopped outside the school doors.

She hadn't noticed the building clouds above her. Was one forming an anvil?

"Please, no storms," Wendy said as she walked into the school.

The first thing Mr. Andrews told everyone to do was to write an essay titled, "What I Would Do If I Could Do Anything I Wanted During Spring Break."

Wendy tapped her pencil against her nose and thought. Anything? Would she

41

spend the week on a storm chasing tour with the Weather Warriors? Jessica could take tons of pictures and Dennis would find new weather experiments. Austin? He'd probably be trying to find a way to fly a kite in a lightning storm.

Or maybe she'd visit the National Severe Storms Lab in Oklahoma with her dad.

Then she smiled. She wrote, "If I could do anything I wanted during spring break, I would do something amazing to keep Mr. Andrews from moving away."

When their time was up, everyone passed them to the front desks to Mr. Andrews.

Then he announced, "Every teacher has chosen five students to help set up for the carnival. You will leave now and return to class after lunch. To make it fair, I drew five names randomly. These students, please go stand by the door."

Wendy held her breath.

"Dennis Galloway," Mr. Andrews said.

Wendy clapped as Dennis passed her desk. He clasped his hands together and raised them in a victory salute.

"Martha Fenner and Austin Scott," Mr. Andrews said.

Wendy's heart pounded. She looked at Jessica, who had her fingers crossed. All of them.

Mr. Andrews smiled and said, "And Wendy Peters and Gabe Sanchez."

Wendy squealed, then glanced at Jessica and mouthed, "Sorry." She couldn't believe Jessica wouldn't be helping them, while Austin-the-weird would be running around in circles.

Wendy stood up and moved close to Mr. Andrews. She whispered, "Turn on your weather radio. Please let Mrs. Stuard know, too. It looks like rain."

Mr. Andrews stared at her. "Tornadoes again?"

She shrugged. "Maybe not. But maybe bad stuff. Or maybe nothing."

Wendy followed her classmates into the hall. Kids from other classrooms were standing in the hall, too. Then Mr. Rodriguez, the vice principal, motioned for them all to line up. He led them past the cafetorium, past the office, and out the side doors like he was the pied piper.

"Wow," Dennis said.

The rides had already been put together and sat in silence, ready to move up and down and all around. Kids from the other fifth grade classes were helping to carry the booths across the grass and line them up in a giant *U*.

There were bottles to be set up for kids to throw softballs at. Little plastic ducks

to be put into a metal tub that would be filled with water. Foam disks to throw through holes cut out in pieces of wood and basketballs to stack beside a tall hoop.

Wendy grabbed the life-size picture of Mr. Andrews and set him right beside the entrance to the rides. Everyone would see him there.

"Look at that!" Austin shouted. The dunking booths had been put together. Austin picked up an imaginary ball and threw it at the button that would knock the teachers into the water.

Wendy shivered. Good thing it was going to be a warm day on Friday. She looked up and frowned. There were a lot of clouds. She could see cumulus clouds and a few cumulus castellanus clouds. They were piling high like towers on a castle. That meant a lot of air movement.

Weathermouth said he thought the rain would wait until Saturday. She hoped he was right. Storms sometimes snuck up suddenly. Wendy loved watching storm clouds, but not now. Not until the carnival was over.

The clouds were high and seemed to be building like cotton candy. Wendy squinted through her glasses. This time, she felt sure one cloud had started forming an anvil. That meant a supercell storm.

As the wind started to blow harder, everyone moved faster. One of the teachers moved the bottles from the Break-a-Bottle booth and laid them in a box inside the booth.

Wendy had just finished setting up a sign when she heard thunder and felt the first drops of rain. Everyone grabbed things that might blow around and put them inside booths or under tables.

Wendy loved the rain on her face. She looked up and closed her eyes.

"Ow!" someone shouted.

Wendy flinched when something smacked her on the forehead. She opened her eyes to see bits of pea-sized hail bouncing on the ground around her.

"Everyone back inside!" a teacher shouted.

Wendy and the other kids pushed into the dry school. Just as the door shut, Wendy watched the hail come down.

It was getting faster.

And bigger.

CHAPTER 8

By the time Wendy and the others got back to Mr. Andrews's class, the hail was like a blizzard outside the windows. A few pieces bounced against the glass and some of the kids screamed.

"Stay away from the windows," Mr. Andrews said. He glanced at Wendy. "I should've had the weather radio on sooner. Mrs. Stuard was out of the office. We wouldn't have let you kids go out if we'd have listened to the warnings."

Wendy said, "It's okay. I was so excited about the carnival, I didn't think to turn mine on this morning either."

Thunder rattled the windows.

"Let's have our reading time now," Mr. Andrews said.

The reading station was in the corner of the room, opposite of the windows.

"What about the carnival stuff?" Jessica asked.

Wendy stared at the hail. From where she was sitting, it was hard to see the size of the hail. But it looked like it was marble, even golf-ball sized. She knew that could do a lot of damage.

Mr. Andrews shook his head. "Let's just hope it stops quickly and there isn't any damage. I know all you kids put a lot of hard work into the carnival."

Wendy couldn't say anything. Her throat felt tight. What if the carnival was cancelled or Mrs. Stuard decided to wait for weeks? And if Mr. Andrews moved away during spring break? He wouldn't see how much everyone at Circleville Elementary loved him.

By the time they read the last chapter of *Tales of Viking Explorers*, the storm had stopped.

Everyone looked toward the windows. Mr. Andrews nodded at them. "I know you want to see what it looks like outside. Go ahead."

Jessica was the first at the window. She had her camera ready and was taking pictures by the time Wendy pushed through her classmates.

Wendy gasped. The school grounds looked like someone had dropped about a million white marbles on the grass. Some of them looked as big as Ping-Pong balls.

She pressed her head against the glass, but she couldn't see the field area where they had set up for the carnival.

The intercom speaker crackled. "Will those students from fifth grade who helped set up the carnival please meet at the west doors," Mrs. Stuard announced.

Mr. Andrews said, "Okay, those who went before can leave, but please stay with the supervising teachers. And Jessica, do you have your camera with you?"

Jessica held it up. "I always have it."

"Good. Please go with them and record any damage," Mr. Andrews said.

Wendy grabbed Jessica by the arm. They followed the others into the hall and lined up with the rest of the helpers. When they came to the doors that led outside to the field, Mr. Rodriguez was waiting.

"We need your help cleaning up. Please don't touch any glass or pick up any boards with nails. Let the adults do that."

He opened the door and everyone filed out.

Wendy gasped. It wasn't the hail covering the ground or the tree limbs hanging off trees that made her want to cry. The carnival looked like someone had attacked it with a giant baseball bat.

Wendy crunched over the hail and just stared at the mess. Many of the booths had holes in them. She wished they had used thicker wood. She could see dents on the rides. The seats on the giant swing ride were covered in hail. The Break-a-Bottle booth was full of broken bottles.

"Oh no!" Wendy shouted. She ran to the life-size picture of Mr. Andrews. It was lying on the ground, covered in hail. Large pieces had gone right through the cardboard.

Jessica moved around the field and took pictures of everything.

"What are we going to do now?" Wendy asked Dennis.

"I don't know. Looks like the carnival is over," Dennis said.

Wendy closed her eyes. It couldn't be over. Mr. Andrews said he was packing everything during spring break. This was their only chance to convince him to stay.

Then Wendy's eyes popped open. She snapped her fingers. "Dennis, do you have hail experiments and ideas in your notebook?"

A smile spread across Dennis's face and he nodded. Then, he pulled out his notebook.

Wendy said, "Come on, let's get the others."

They found Jessica and Austin and then went to find Mrs. Stuard. It was time for the Weather Warriors to save the Spring Carnival.

CHAPTER 9

Weather Warriors to the Rescue

On Friday morning, three warriors met together in the office and waited for Mrs. Stuard.

"She'll be back in a moment," the secretary said. "She's talking to the food venders."

Wendy thanked the secretary and motioned for Jessica and Austin.

"Do you think she got it all done?" Jessica asked.

Austin shook a small ice chest. "I brought my stuff. See!" He opened the lid and they peeked inside.

"Perfect," Wendy said.

Dennis burst into the office, his breath coming in gasps. "I checked outside and the rides are almost fixed. There were just a bunch of dents on stuff. They said they've already done all the safety checks on the merry-go-round, Scrambler, swings, and Ferris wheel."

"Great," Wendy said. She pulled out a notebook. On the cover were cut-outs of different sized hail stones. She opened it to a page titled, *Spring Hail Carnival To-Do List*. Her mom always kept a to-do list of things to get done.

She checked off where it read, *Rides repaired*.

Byron Jenkins walked into the office. "Hey, I got some really big pieces of hail."

Jessica followed Byron outside. There, a bunch of kids were all waiting with ice chests. Jessica lined them up and told them to open the lids. She took pictures and they quickly closed the chests again.

When they were done, Jessica returned to Mrs. Stuard's office. When Mrs. Stuard squeezed through the door, she motioned Wendy and the Weather Warriors to follow her into her office.

Wendy, Jessica, Dennis, and Austin followed Mrs. Stuard.

She fell into her chair and sighed. "Whew, I've been busy all morning, but I think we're ready. Several of the parents came last night and rebuilt some of the game booths. I have the tables set up that you asked for and new signs made for them."

Wendy shook Mrs. Stuard's hand. "Thanks. I know this will be the best Spring Carnival ever. And Mr. Andrews won't . . ." She covered her mouth with her hand.

Mrs. Stuard winked. "I think I know what's going on here." She motioned to the door. "You've been given the morning off from classes. It's only a half day anyway and then the carnival will start. Mr. Rodriguez will help you get everything ready."

Wendy felt like skipping out of the office. How many kids went into the principal's office and came out smiling?

Mr. Rodriguez was waiting for them.

Wendy said, "Hi, Mr. Rodriguez. The Weather Warriors know all about hail. Did you know that it can fall as fast as 100 miles per hour? If my dad drove that fast he'd get a speeding ticket!"

Mr. Rodriguez laughed. He nudged Dennis. "That girl's head is full of weather facts."

He led them outside to the field. Wendy clapped her hands. The parents had done a great job repairing the booths. Most of them still had dents in the wood, but that made it perfect for the Weather Warriors new plan for the carnival theme.

There were three tables set up with new signs.

GUESS THE HAILSTONE SIZE!

YOUR PICTURE WITH A HAILSTONE!

EXPERIMENTS WITH HAIL!

"Okay," Wendy said. "Let's get to work."

CHAPTER 10

An Icy Carnival

"**C**ome guess the hailstone size and you are a winner!" Wendy shouted.

She stood behind her table surrounded by small ice chests full of hailstones of all sizes. She hoped they wouldn't melt before the carnival ended.

Classes had just let out for the carnival. Teachers worked at game booths where kids could throw hailstones through holes. Buckets of golf balls and softballs could be bought for a quarter.

There were popcorn balls for sale, but the sign had been changed to Hail Balls.

Jessica was busy taking pictures of kids holding the biggest hailstones that students and teachers brought from home.

Dennis stood with five kids watching him. He pointed to one girl and gave her a small piece of hail. "Now, if you drop this quarter size hailstone through the foil over that bowl, it makes a big hole. But if you raise your hand higher and throw this softball sized piece, see what happens to the foil and the bowl?"

Austin bounced up and down on a mini-trampoline at his booth. "Come over here and be a bouncy hailstone!" he shouted.

Wendy grinned when she heard the *ping* of a bell. She looked across the field where someone had just dumped Mr. Andrews into the water tank. She could hear him laughing.

Mrs. Stuard walked through the carnival with a bullhorn. "If everyone will come to the west side of the field, Mr. Andrews and Miss Holland will judge the Best Dressed Hailstone Contest."

Wendy clapped her hands. She grabbed Jessica from her booth and yelled for Dennis.

They pushed through the crowd to a long table that was filled with pieces of hail. That morning kids had decorated them with doll clothes and pipe cleaners and tiny little hats that kept falling off.

Mr. Andrews and Miss Holland had changed into dry clothes, but their hair was still wet. Wendy was glad it was a sunny day.

Wendy nudged the kid next to her and said, "Isn't it amazing that we had hail just yesterday and now it's a beautiful day?"

The kid just stared at her like she was crazy.

"They're judging now," Jessica said.

Wendy peered around the kids in front of her. Mr. Andrews and Miss Holland were bending down to look at each hailstone in the long row. They laughed and pointed at their favorites. Wendy had never seen Mr. Andrews smile so big.

Finally, Mr. Andrews cleared his throat. "This has been a difficult contest to judge. Especially since the contestants keep melting and losing their costumes. But I think Miss Holland and I have chosen three winners."

Miss Holland took a deep breath. She tugged at the sleeves of her pink shirt. She tapped her pink earrings. Wendy had never seen so much pink on one person. Even her pants were pink!

"The third-place prize goes to Teresa Forbes from Mrs. Halley's third grade room for her Abe Lincoln hailstone."

A squeal came from the crowd as a pig-tailed girl stepped out. She took the hailstone with the beard and the tall black hat from Mr. Andrews. Then Miss Holland gave her a yellow ribbon.

"And in second place, we have Justin Holland's pig hailstone. He is in Mrs. Baker's first grade class."

Wendy laughed as Mr. Andrews held out the pink piece of hail that had a curly pink pipe cleaner wrapped around the end. No wonder Miss Holland chose it. She smiled at him as she gave him a red ribbon.

Mr. Andrews cleared his throat again. "And our first-place winner is from my own class," he said. "First place goes to

Austin Scott for his amazing dragon hailstone."

Austin nearly flew out of the crowd. He skidded into the table. Everyone yelled as the decorated hailstones all wobbled and rolled.

"Oops, sorry," he said.

Mr. Andrews set a large hailstone in Austin's left hand. It had been painted green and had paper wings that fluttered when Austin moved it up and down. Somehow he'd attached a long, thin neck and the dragon's head had an open mouth. Just as Austin held it up, one wing fell off.

"Great job," Miss Holland said as she placed a blue ribbon in Austin's right hand.

Wendy gave Austin a thumbs-up. He might not be a big weather expert, but he sure added something unusual to the Weather Warriors.

The crowd scattered back to the activities. Wendy ran over to Mr. Andrews. "Wow, you did a great job of judging. You know why? Because you're the best teacher in all of Circleville Elementary."

She put her hand over her mouth when Miss Holland walked over to them. Miss Holland smiled. "I have to agree. If I were in fifth grade right now, I'd want him for my teacher, too."

Mr. Andrews squeezed water from his wet ponytail. "Thanks. I do love teaching. But it's hard to pass up a chance to be vice principal. Especially after the news I got today."

Wendy said, "News? What news?"

Mr. Andrews folded his arms. "You'll have to wait like everyone else. I'll make an announcement during the king and queen's closing speeches at the end of the carnival."

Wendy watched as the king and queen walked away.

CHAPTER 11

The New Announcement

Wendy wished the carnival could go on forever. But it was almost time for the buses to come. The hailstones had all melted and the rides were shutting down.

Wendy didn't know if the Weather Warriors and the kids at Circleville had done enough to make Mr. Andrews stay.

"Smile," Jessica shouted. She pointed her camera at Wendy. "You look too serious after all this fun."

Wendy walked beside Jessica to the small stage where Mrs. Stuard, Mr. Rodriguez, Mr. Andrews, and Miss Holland were standing.

"Sorry. It was a lot of fun. I'm just afraid of Mr. Andrews's next announcement," Wendy said.

Jessica held out her camera. "Look at all the great pictures I got of people. And I took pictures of all the dressed-up hailstones before the contest judging. And look, here are some pictures of Mr. Andrews and Miss Holland being dunked and . . ."

"Hey, what's this one?" Wendy asked. She pointed to a picture on the camera screen.

"Oh, that's Mr. Andrews talking to some man. He came right before the hail contest judging. He talked to Mr. Andrews for a long time, then they shook hands. See, I got a picture of them shaking," Jessica said.

Wendy stared at the picture. Mr. Andrews was smiling in it. The other man was smiling. She wondered if it was someone from the school in Arizona. She decided she didn't like the man in the suit.

Dennis waved to them from the back of the crowd. When Wendy looked on the stage, she could see the man in the suit standing behind it. Mrs. Stuard was talking with him and smiling.

Jessica and Wendy moved closer when Mrs. Stuard walked over to the microphone that had been set up on the stage.

"We've come to the end of this year's Spring Carnival. It wasn't exactly as we'd first planned, but I hope everyone had a great time," she said.

The kids shouted, whistled, and clapped. Wendy couldn't help but smile.

"And once again, our group of Weather Warriors—Wendy, Dennis, Jessica, and Austin—saved the day by coming up with this fun idea to rescue the carnival after the hailstorm," Mrs. Stuard said.

Everyone cheered. Mrs. Stuard held up her hands. "Now, before we leave for spring break, Mr. Andrews, our Spring Carnival King, has an announcement."

Mr. Andrews took the microphone and said, "As many of you know, I announced to my class a few days ago that I was taking a job as vice principal next year at a new school. Because it's out of state, my plan was to leave right away and get set up there."

Wendy scowled. Austin shouted, "Boo!"

Mr. Andrews pulled a ruler from his jacket and tapped it on his head.

Everyone laughed, but the kids in Mr. Andrews's class knew that meant to be quiet.

"Since last night, my plans have changed."

Wendy gasped. She leaned forward. "Quiet," she said to the kids around her.

Mr. Andrews cleared his throat. "I have not signed my contract in Arizona yet. I was going to do that on Monday. I've decided not to sign it."

Wendy grabbed Jessica's arm. She jumped up and down. She shouted.

"But, I will still be leaving Circleville Elementary," Mr. Andrews shouted into the microphone.

Wendy stopped jumping. She stopped shouting.

"Yesterday I got a call from Mr. Thomas, the principal assigned to the new middle school being built in Circleville." Mr. Andrews pointed to the man in the suit. "He asked me to become the vice principal for the new school. This morning, I accepted. I'll be finishing the year here. Next year, I'll see you fifth graders at the new school."

Wendy gasped. Mr. Andrews's announcement couldn't have been any better. He would still be their teacher for the rest of the year. And even better, he would be at the middle school, too.

Mr. Andrews held the microphone up once more. "I've never had so much fun after a hailstorm. How could I leave you before the year ends? I look forward to seeing some of you next year and all of you at Cyclone Middle School as the years go by."

Wendy's mouth dropped open.

She turned to Dennis and Jessica. "Did you hear that name?"

Wendy jumped up and down and shouted, "Hail to the King of Circleville Elementary!"

Other kids started shouting, some adding, "Hail to the Queen!"

Wendy grabbed Jessica's camera and took a picture of everyone standing on the stage. Even the man in the suit.

"Hail to King Andrews," she whispered. "And hail to the hailstorm."

She bowed to one small piece of hail left sitting in the shade of the oak tree.

Did You Know?

- Hail is much more common along mountain ranges because mountains force winds upward. This makes the updrafts more intense and hail more likely.

- Large hailstones can fall at speeds faster than 100 miles per hour (161 km/h).

- The largest hailstone recovered in the United States fell in Aurora, Nebraska, on June 22, 2003. It was seven inches (18 cm) wide. That's as large as a soccer ball!

- Most hailstorms happen between March and June. States that have the most frequent hail are Kansas, Colorado, Oklahoma, Nebraska, Texas, and Wyoming.

DENNIS'S Favorite Experiments

NAMING HAILSTONES

When you hear a report about hail, it is compared in size to certain things. This experiment will help you get an idea of how hail gets named.

YOU NEED:

- A frozen pea
- A golf ball
- A baseball
- A softball
- A quarter
- A penny
- A grapefruit
- A Ping-Pong ball
- A marble
- A tennis ball